Sugar & Smiles

Flairs and Glairs

Publication House

"Sugar and Smiles"

ISBN No: " 9789391302177"
1st Edition
Language – English and Hindi

Flairs and Glairs
Publication House
Regd. Under MSME Act.

Disclaimer

This is a work of fiction and solely represent the thoughts of the corresponding authors of the articles.
Our editors have tried their best to edit the content of all the authors and check the plagiarism.
All the write-ups in this book are unique and are only published in this book.
In case any plagiarism or error is found, only the author is responsible alone, and not the publisher or the Compilers.

Cover Designing and Book Formatting
Shubham Shah and Ishani Agarwal

Acknowledgment

Dear Almighty, thank you for blessing me with the power and zeal to be able to complete this Anthology.

Also, Thank You dear parents, for trusting in me, and letting me work whenever I wanted. My family is the one who supported me for what I am today.

When it comes to this, Anthology, I would like to start with Thanking the Co -Authors, without your help and support, I would have never been able to complete it.

Thank you all of you, for being there. Much Love to all of you. I am glad to see you all standing by me.

Co Author

Shubham Shah (Founder Flairs and Glairs)
Ishani Agarwal (Co-Founder Flairs and Glairs)
Shivangi Jaiswal (Compiler)

1.Ms. Ishrat Jahan Noormohammed Khan
2.Bhavika Dhiraj Sindhi
3.Muskan Gupta
4.Priyanka K. Tiwari
5.Riya Srivastava
6.Arnab Dasgupta
7.Barsha Das
8.Rudra Gupta
9.Roopali Purohit
10.Rutba Qayoom
11.Anwesa Chakraborty
12.Gayatri Sharma
13.Sayandeep Patra
14.Ketan B Jadhav
15.Keerthana

Shubham Shah

(Founder - Flairs and Glairs)

Shubham Shah, an entrepreneur at "Flairs & Glairs" a brand with dynamics in events organizing and cultural educational pan INDIA, is a 26yrs old guy who recently has entered the digital platform of imprinting emotions. He has initiated with his own open mic platform to help budding poets and aspiring writers under his brand named as "Teekhe Zasbaaat"

He is a commerce graduate from the Bhagalpur City of Bihar.
He states Writing has impersonated him since childhood and he has now been writing for over a decade!
Cooking, on the other hand, is his passion! He also mentions, trying out new things just tickles him!
When asked sir, Why SPICY EMOTIONS?
He smiled and added, "agar jasbaat teekhe na ho toh wo jasbaat kahan" Spices are all that blends! So do his words!
As a chef, he presents to you his dish! Hot and freshly served! Taste it! Feel it! Enjoy it! You can also find his writing in the Book "Teekhe Zasbaaat" and 50+ Co -authored anthologies. With his passion to explore opportunities across Platforms, he is working with keen dev otion and We wish him all the very best for his future ventures.
He is Featured in the International Magazine DeMode for his upcoming solo novel.
He is Approved by Ne8x for its Lit Fest, and is a Golden Star Awards 2020 Winner.
He is a India Book of Records Holder for his Anthology Satrang, and has the Grandmaster title by Asia Book of Records, for the same.
He has also been featured in Prabhat Khabar, Dainik Jagran, and a lot of other Newspapers in Bihar for his achievements.
He has been a proud co-author to
India Book Of Records (Title- Black)
World Book Of Records (Title -15 Wonders of Poetries)
India Book Of Records (Title - Aaina)
Vajra World Records Holder (Title - Gustakhi Maaf Hai)
High Range of Records Holder (Title - Gustakhi Maaf Hai)
Indian Book of Records
(Title - Road from Worst to Best)

Share your reviews on his

INSTAGRAM

@spicy_emotions
@shubham4shah

Or via email on

shubham2shah@gmail.com

To stay tuned to his work and opportunities follow his business Handles

INSTAGRAM   FACEBOOK   YOUTUBE

@flairsandglairs
@teekhezasbaaat

WEBSITE:

https://flairsandglairs.in/
https://flairsandglairs.com/

Ishani Agarwal

(Co-Founder- Flairs and Glairs)

Ishani Agarwal hails from the City of Joy, Kolkata.
She is the co -founder of her Community "Teekhe Zasbaaat"
and Flairs and Glairs Publication.
Been a Compiler for 45+ Anthologies, she is in the process for
more. Co-authored in 150+ Anthologies. She is a India Book
of Records Holder, a Vajra World Records Holder, a High
Range of Records Holder, an OMG Book of Records Holder,
a Bravo Record holder, a Forever Star Book of World Records
and an Indian Book of Records Holder.
Approved by Ne8x for its Lit Fest 2020, and Literary Icon
2020. Also a Golden Star Awards Winner 2020.
She has also been award ed with India Star Republic Award
2021, a part of She Awards by Awards Arc and Winner of Nari
Samman 2021 by Literoma.

She is also selected as Best Achiever of the Year by AwardsArc and Most Challenging Compiler Award by Spectrum Awards.
She got her first solo Published,a solo Compilation consisting of first 750 contents of hers, titled "Hand That Burnt While Healing".

She has been featured by the National Magazine "Taree Zameen Par" with the title 'unstoppable'.
Also featured in the International Magazine DeMode for her upcoming solo novel, she is proud to write on social issues, and is happy with the love she is receiving.
Connect with her on Instagram: @Ishani_agarwal_quotes / @compilations_so_far

Shivangi Jaiswal
(Compiler)

Shivangi Jaiswal is a Content Writer from Kolkata. Executive Head at "Flairs & Glairs" brand with dynamics in events organizing and cultural educational pan INDIA. Organizer at "The Glittering Fables" Writing Community. She is a B. Com Honors graduate. Certified in Stocks & Short Selling as well as Certified in Digital Marketing student.
She is an Indian Book of Record Holder.

Approved by Ne8x for its Lit Fest 2020 for the Author of the Year 2020 and the Real Hero's Title 2020. Also, a Warrior of Change Awardee 2021

She loves to bring smiles and happiness to many faces, so she is into Social service.

Traveler, Teacher, Meditator, Dancer, Singer, Instrument Player. She loves to play guitar and harmonium. Also been awarded in many events for winning many categories Been a Public Speaker she has taken part in many events and nailed it. Been a great Advisor to many. She has also been crowned for winning Miss Great Podium 2020 Title in the category Modelling recently. Sports freak of Swimming and Badminton with a passion so strong. Since, past one year she has started her writing journey.

She writes so that many people can connect with their stories and get positive hopes. She thinks " Every story is unique so embrace yourself to the best". She is a writer by day and a reader by night. Been a Complier of 3 2+ Anthologies, and in process for more, also Co - authored 1 20+ anthologies. Shivangi is an old soul with young eyes, a vintage heart, and a beautiful mind."

You can follow her work:
Instagram
@the_knockingvibe
@house_of_compilations

First Kiss

First kiss beneath the moon,
under the sky you and I.
I wish to stop this time.
The feeling that has found unexpectedly,
and turned by world so great.

Oh, please remain with me, so that
I can savour you again and hold you in my smile.
When life has brought me nothing but tears,
you gave me reasons to smile.
I sometime wonder how can someone make you smile in
trouble also.
I think life is just like that, a beautiful rejoice.

I learned to smile because of you.
Your smiles are heaven with a glee.
An unbelieving smile flit on us
eyes when we see each other.
My love, heaven has tied our knot.
With an everlasting bond forever.

To My Future Love.

We may have crossed same paths, not knowing each other.
There would be a moment, where we are together but unknown
from each other.

May be one is crying over things, and other is smiling in
rejoice.
There might be a moment where we both are broken, but we
are learning from our mistake.

So that when we meet, we are mature Enough to handle our
relationship.
I'm on the way to meet you soon, I might be a bit late. But be
patient.

I have always waited   to meet you at the right time. And I
promise to be there with you soon. Our hearts will meet soon
and cast a magic spell of love.

One day the stars will also align to spell our name together.
Dreams will soon come true.

Forgiveness Is Hard.

Forgiveness is a gift,
which only a few deserve.
Mistakes happen, but learn to accept it
A wrong word can shatter everything,
where sometimes you can never gain forgiveness again.

It's not easy to forgive someone
when you are hurt or betrayed.
You try to forgive them but your
heart doesn't allow you to do.
Because once the pieces are
broken you cannot mend them again.

The marks on it goes with time.
And it's very hard to let go things.
Never hurt someone you love the most,
that it ruins their happiness
And at last forgiveness is also of no use.

Learn to love,
Learn to forgive
Learn to make a powerful bond
Life is small
Be happy and live happy.

(4)

Bahut Pyaare lag rahe ho,
Na jane kyu jab se Dekha hai
Teri Ankho mein

Kuch alag sa hai, kuch naya sa hai,
Bahut Haseen Lag Raha Hai.

Nigahon se jo Katal kiya aapne,
Voh Lamha Bahut Azeez Lag Raha hai.

Tujhse mil ke humne khud ko paya,
Tere ishq ka nasha kuch aisa char ke chaya.

Ruk gayi Sansei, tham gaya sama.
Ab aapki aur kya baatein kare?
Apse pyaara koi ho hi nahi sakta.

Burn Souls.

I often wonder,

Why did we draw a line between us?
Why did things change from good to worse?

We holded the knife knowing it would cut us,
The fire inside will burn us.

We tried to fix it,
But couldn't justify our foolishness.

Droplets pouring down from our eyes,
when the knife pierces our hearts.
We could feel the pain, Crying out.

Why? Why? Love me.
Please don't stop loving me.

But who knew loving a wild thing was never easy?
In return you burn yourself only.

How Do You Know He Is The Right One For You?

The one who makes me complete.
The one who held my hand in all situations.
The one who understands me more than myself.
The one who believes in me.

The ones who listen to my soul.
The one who is my life.
The one who turns off my nightmares.
The one who brings light of hope.
The one who would look into my eyes and make me feel the love inside.

The one who would share all his feelings with me.
The one who would stand by me in good and bad face.
The one who would make me feel safe in his arms.
The one who would make me realize that yes, I'm his soul mate.

True love really matters a lot.
So, I'll be waiting for t he right, Because you're my biggest happiness.

Ms. Ishrat Jahan Noormohammed Khan

Ms Ishrat jahan khan is a passionate Teacher and a Writer she loves reading and writing. Loving and caring is her hobby. And keep learning and accept the positive suggestion is her quality.

She belongs to North India and stays at Ulhasnagar (Maharashtra).

Loves humanity always.

At present she is Assistant Head Mistress for secondary and higher secondary section at S.A.C.H.S.S and Project Head at Flairs and Flairs.

Meri Lifeline Ban Gai

Mere do parivar ban gaye
Mere jindagi ka hissa ban gaye

Ek mera school S.A.C.H.S.S
Aur duja mera F & G

Ye kaise hua samaj na saki mai
Kaise hua samaj na saki mai

Par Deere Deere ye dono
Mere dhadkan ka hissa ban gaye

Lots of love to S.A.C.H.S.S and F & G family

Sky Is Your

Keep smiling life is less
Make it best it like a chess
Pride is to be kept
But love is to be kept

Happiness is soul
You don't scroll
Make it happy with dignity
So that you have integrity

Make it a sugar smile
That should be your style
And no need to shy
If you are true then your is sky

Life Should Be Cool

Life should be cool
Let people call you fool
You don't become harsh
Or else be ready to crash

Happiness should be motto
And life should be totto
Meaning of life should be happiness
Let the price for its craziness

Make the things transplant
And it should be well plant
No one can judge you
Or else they will nudge you

Smile and Sugar

Smile and sugar
No need to fear
Someone will be dear
Who will always be nearby?

They will make you sweet
So that you can beat
Let the mind filled with heat
But style should be beneath

Smile should be sugar
Without any figure
Love should be base
Care should be craze

A Small Initiative to Protect Our Identity

पापा मै शादी नहीं करूंगी !

पापा मै शादी नहीं करूंगी
दहेज की कीमत पर बिल्कुल नहीं.
पापा मैं शादी नहीं करूंगी
दहेज की कीमत पर बिल्कुल नहीं.

इस कीमत पर शादी करके
आपके जिंदगी ,मेहनत और शीख को बर्बादी नहीं करूंगी पापा

पापा मैं शादी नहीं करूंगी

जिंदगी भर बहोत मेहनत से
 आपने पैसा कमाया है
हम सब को सफल बनाया
पाई पाई करके प्रॉपर्टी बनाई
कैसे यह घर बनवाया है
दहेज के बहाने
आप की प्रॉपर्टी पर नजर डालने वालों की
आबादी नहीं करूंगी

ना पापा मैं शादी नहीं करूंगी

इनकी बली नही चड़ुंगी पापा
गैस सिलेंडर से नहीं जलूँगी पापा
अखबारों के पन्ने नही बनूँगी पापा
बेटी आपकी ही रहूंगी पापा

आजकल बुढ़ापे में भी
आत्मनिर्भर होना मजबूरी है
मुझे दहेज में जो पैसा दोगे ना
आपके फ्यूचर के लिए वह बहुत जरूरी है आपका सहारा बन पाऊं
ना बन पाऊं
बुढ़ापे का सहारा छीन कर
जल्दी नहीं करूंगी

पापा मैं शादी नहीं करूंगी
आपने मुझे पढ़ाया लिखाया
पंख दिए काबिल बनाया
उड़ने को आसमान दिया
 रंग दिए जीने को
दहेज में एक भी रुपया मैं ना ले जाऊंगी आपको और मां को रोड
पर लाकर
अपना घर में कैसे बसाऊंगी
आपके दिए विचोरो की......
बर्बादी नहीं करूंगी

मैं इन रस्मो को तोड़ूंगी पापा
हर पिता की उमीद को जोड़ूंगी पापा
गलत को बढ़ावा नही दूंगी पापा
बेटी हु बेटी ही रहूंगी पापा

पापा मैं शादी नहीं करूंगी
नहीं इस कीमत पर नहीं ...
पापा मैं शादी नहीं करूंगी
नहीं इस कीमत पर नहीं

Bhavika Dhiraj Sindhi

Bhavika Dhiraj Sindhi a creative writer. She belongs to Turkey an Indian writing from abroad due to her passion in writing. a curious girl A wanderer who   likes to explore new things and places a hardheaded but softhearted She uses her pen as a best friend to spea   k her feelings... Believes only love can make this place a better to survive...!

Life as The Senses

Life is all about senses...!
A sense of style,
A sense of proportion,
A sense of beauty,
A sense of grace...!
Life is nothing without these,
Senses of feel, vision, hear, smell, taste...!
The Butterflies in the stomach ..
The blank mind,
The trembling words,
The vanished common sense,
The eleope to vivid sphere,
The swirling felicity,
The placid moment,
The tranquilized smile widens,
It's the crush o n someone meant to be special...!

How Life Feels Like...?

Shining like a diamond,
Dazzling in the sun shine,
People could just see the cream of the shine,
Diamond is formed after intense pressure,
Aggrandizing the look,
Somedays are low key,
Doesn't mean it's an end,
Road tripping and having a pause,
Tired,
Doesn't mean the trip is over,
The adventure must go on,
The new day arrives,
Bloom glowingly,
Dull are dawn and dusk too,
Yet so pleasant and soothing,
Peace is aspiration,
To prove your w orth to anyone,
Isn't required,
Instead, it's the time to utterly and absolutely walk away,
Take some deep and fresh breath,
Feel the best of you,
And it has a different glow,
Emotionally draining,
Robs you of the little wonders of life...
It doubles your workload,
just to smile and participate in the shallowness of the world
around you.
It will open your senses
but then you are deeper
than those you interact with,
That makes you feel more alone...
So smile,
Feel yourself,

Love yourself,
Important is to grow,
To the damb fire you are...!

When Life Hears Like?

Adventures are my kind of life,
Mountains are my best friend,
Going high is what it makes me realise,
Climbing high falling down,
Picking myself up,
To the mountains I shout
The echoes hit me back,
Just like the karma,
What goes around comes back,
Is all that life hears like,
The shattering of a heart,
When broken,
Is the loudest quiet ever you hear ever in your life,
The two big ears are just like the gateway in the garden,
You hear something,
You roam around just like you roam the globe,
While exit you have experience,
And throw your self out to be in the garden,
Just like how you throw things your ears hear the
unnecessary thoughts,
Hearing your inner self help you grow,
Just like the music is the best therapy for life,
When upset the music encourages you,
When happy partying with the music and be the leader just
like you aree and with your life,
You listen what you wish to and act accordingly,
Your blessed with this hearing,
The one the creator of the universe,
Hears your silent prayers..!
Don't be naive,
Just listen,
But don't lose your own voice..!

How Life Sees Like ...?

The magic of new beginnings,
The new days sunshine,
The rays of hope,
Giving you energy,
Too look the things in a completely different manner on your end,
Something's gets crystal clear,
With the time as the water,
Looking in the mirror,
I realised I'm growing,
Gaining strength,
Learning lessons from my mistake and pain,
I see the pride in myself,
Realising I m not a victim,
Instead a fighter,
The scars are seen by many,
Yet understood by few,
Tied my eyes with a black ribbon,
Was left in a garden,
The only day I realised,
This beautiful little place becomes hell,
Without the colours,
The beautiful colourful tulip,
The red lovely rose,
The sun rays hitting the leaves and the dew drops,
A highlighter it felt ,
Everything would be worthless,
If in real-life would-be spectre,
Always trusted what we see,
But it's really traumatic,
When we feel sugar and it turns to be salt,
Be careful,
It may hurt you,

Everyone wants to be someone's sun,
To light up someone's life,
Definitely none wants to be the moon,
To brighten you up in your darkest hour..!
The torch in the dark ,
Are the rare gems in your life..!

How Life Smells Like...?

Life is a journey, Walking in the garden, Smelling the first rain, The fragrance of which warm hugs from the landscape Smell of the Peteichor, Feels like a moss in the woods, I like the baggy jumpers and My faithfully beat up boots Protecting me from the muddy soil, No less then the problems In my life Getting drenched in the rain Experiencing the best of it Returning home, The warm water baths is just like your warm hugs, You shampoo your hair the smell is my drug, I feel you all around floating in the ir, You were the new book in my life, The aroma of which made me crazy Turned to yellow pages now, Yet each day when I open it smells extraordinarily new, Each day I open yet it smells extraordinary, None thought to bottle up..! The hot tea made by you , Aroma of which lingers around, That of the freshly cut bower, Redolent with the rich cinnamony sweet barbecue smell of the muffin, You add the bonbon to my quintessence..! Marvellous is the aroma of the salty water, As the breeze brushes off our face The fi re woods in the camp fire, Near the shore, And the barbecue is the cherry on the cake, The flavour makes me lost in you , The bouquet of wine, Is like the solution to my life..! The night stary with the light moonlight, The calm to my senses, Smelling your skin, The daisy delled, Smelling the seas, The soul is infused, Feeling the sky, Making my spirits fly..! Passing the whole night beside you, Just the smell of the summers, Make me fall more for you, The savour of soft sunshine, The dews on the leaves, Feels like your soft lips, Mixed beautifully with, The tang of sunshine

How Life Taste Likes...???

Life is a bag of candies, Fondness of sweet, sour, tangy..! Fuel is the food, Fill it with premium thingy, Love your body with dignity, Eating well is the step to victory, No therapy is needed to be wealthy, The emotions it all piles, Some are crunchy, Sometimes it's mushy, Some are soft, Some are tasty, Some are buttery, Some are bitter, Yet all necessary to survive, With the ups and downs of life, Is just like tasting some street foods or somedays the veggies that you hate the most, Nourishing your body to survive in this beautiful life..! People have mood swings and food swings i have mood for food swings Food is my happy place i eat when i am happy sad or mad good food good food & good taste that's all you need to live You earn to get bread and the only thing that helps you live a good life is satisfying tasty food Be it street, restaurant or homemade food, food is my guilty pleasure make me workout fo r more but don't say to me to cut out food it's what i love & the satisfaction The pleasure of perfectly baked mac and cheese pasta the cheesy texture the melted cheese when goes in my mouth makes me feel the happiest and that is all you need on a bad da y to cheer your mood the melting cheese is like the melting my problems, Giving me a power to knock back the problems The best partner to chill, with while watching Netflix you eat its triangle and that is the only love triangle, i love is pizza it's always a perfect end to a weekend , I need no one but this, This is my kinda fun and There's no start to monday or any other day without a magnificent cup of coffee, to kick start my day the first sip of perfectly brewed of caffeine, Hits you on your head, and last but The best thing are deserts be it a cake or chocolate it' just adds sweetness to your life..! Modesty is the mind of taste, Simplicity has been essences of flavour, Enjoying the moment, looking at the sky, Tasting the clouds, Feels to have forev er, Writing my feeds, Tasting the spice twice Elegant is the sparkling diamond,

Adding a daring to your taste...! Not all are blessed with good one, Grab and enjoy the moment...! Choosing a good beverage, A glass of good wine, Making the night memorable, Hangovers are temporary, Drunk stories with a bunch of people Last forever...!

Muskan Gupta

She is Muskan Gupta lives in Ayodhya Uttar Pradesh. She is a writer by situation and want to explore more in the field of writing. She is pursuing graduation f   rom Delhi University. Worked as a co-author in more than thirty anthologies.
She wants to motivate more and more people by her creative writeups.

मुस्कराहट की कोई वजह होती है क्या?

मुस्कराहट की कोई वजह होती है क्या?

तुम छुप -छुप के हसो,ये भी कोई बात होती है क्या?

मुस्कराहट की कोई वजह होती है क्या?

तुम यु नज़रे जो फेरते हो,

बिना बातों के मुस्कान शब्द को टीटोलते हो.

ये भी कोई बात होती है क्या इज़हार करने की?

यु ही मुस्कुरा के चल देना अपने लफ्ज़ो में,

क्या वजह होती है मुस्कराहट की?

शायद हाँ.

वो खुद जगकर मुझे ख़ुशी से हसाना.

वो खुद सपने देखकर मुझे उन सपनो में बाइक पर

घूमाना.

बेटोना बोलकर मुझे प्यार से पुचकारना .शायद उसके प्यार जाताने

का उन्ही में से एक तरीका है. मुस्कुराकर बहुत कुछ बोल जाना,

हुदा के मुस्कराहट की वजह है.

<u>नटखट से वो हमारे पैरो के कदम, जब नन्हे थे हम ...</u>

नटखट से वो हमारे पैरो के कदम, जब नन्हे थे हम ...
छोटी -छोटी उंगलियां ,छोटे- छोटे हमारे नन्हे पैर,
छोटी थी हमारी आखें और छोटे थे शकल से हम खैर...
नटखट से वो हमारे पैरो के कदम, जब नन्हे थे हम...
कुछ ऐसी थी वो मुस्कान की मोह लेती थी सबका दिल ,
कुछ ऐसी थी हमारी मासूमियत की जीत लेती सबका दिल

तभी तो कहती हु...
नटखट से वो हमारे पैरो के कदम, जब नन्हे थे हम ...
वो हमारी नटखट सी बातें और नटखट वाले उम्मंग,
भर देती थी ऐसी स्फूर्ति की लोग हो जाते थे मग्न ..
नटखट से वो हमारे पैरो के कदम, जब नन्हे थे हम ...
वो हमारी बाल्यावस्था के भरम, जब नन्हे थे हम .

<u>"आज कुछ अलग सी बात है "...</u>

आज कुछ अलग सी बात है ...
अलग होते हुए भी ना जाने क्यों ये दुःख के एहसास है.
आज कुछ अलग सी बात है,
मुझे अपने साथ-साथ तुम्हें भी खो देने का एहसास
है ...
मुझसे नाराज़ ना होना अगर मैं हो जाऊ खुद तुमसे दूर खुदा की इसमे
कुछ मजबूरी समझ लेना अगर ना हो पाए एक साथ हम हुज़ूर
आज कुछ अलग सी बात है ...
हम साथ होते हुए भी फ़ोन पर, हमारे घर वाले आज खिलाफ है,
मौत माँगना चाहु तो मौत भी आज खिलाफ है .
आज कुछ अलग सी बात है ....
तुमको याद ना करू तो मेरा दिल खफा होता है,
इन घुटन के आसुओं में तू ही तो मेरा एक लौता है,
पता नहीं तुम्हारे बिना ये पहर कैसे बीतेंगे ,
पर आज हम खुद की बेबसी पर खूब आसु बहाएगे ...
आज कुछ अलग सी बात है...

<u>"आज ये क्या गजब बात है"</u>

आज ये क्या गजब बात है, मेरे अपने आज मेरे साथ है, बिना कुछ
कहे मुझपे खुद से ज्यादा इन्हें विश्वास है, आज ये क्या गजब बात है.
मेरे साथी आज हर हाल में मेरे साथ है, आज ये क्या गजब बात है.
इन्हें इतना भरोसा है मुझ पर जितना इन्हें खुद पर नहीं, मैं ईमान हु
इनका जिन्हें कोई समझता नहीं आज ये क्या गजब बात है, मेरे पराए
भी मेरे साथ है. आज ये क्या गजब बात है.

"मैं इंतज़ार करने वाला लड़का हु"

मैं इंतज़ार करने वाला लड़का हु, तुम इंतज़ार करवाने वाली लड़की हो. मैं साप सीडी में निन्यानबे पर साप से कट जाने वाला लड़का हु, तुम अन्ठान्बे पर आकर एक नंबर लाने वाली लड़की हो मैं सीडी लगाने वाला लड़का हु और तुम सीडी उतारने वाली लड़की हो.मैं प्यार को निभा ले जाने वाला लड़का हु और तुम रिश्तों को संभाल ले जाने वाली लड़की हो मैं प्यार से सब्र करने वाला लड़का हु और तुम प्यार से नचाने वाली लड़की हो ... मैं इंतज़ार करने वाला लड़का हु, तुम इंतज़ार करवाने वाली लड़की हो..

ये कैसा मनुष्य का व्यवहार है?

ये कैसा मनुष्य का व्यवहार है? एक तरफ पूजते है नवरात्र को, तो दूसरी तरफ करते बेटियों का तिरस्कार है, ये कैसा मनुष्य का व्यवहार है? माताए और बेटियां मिलकर बढाती देशो में सम्मान है पर फिर भी ना जाने क्यों? कुछ स्थानो में माताए और बेटियां को मिलता ना कभी जीवन में उच्च स्तर का सम्मान है आखिर क्यों.? आज ये कैसा होता जा रहा मनुष्य का व्यवहार है? सवालों में दिन निकल जाएगे, पर रास्ते हमें खुद ही निकालने है, कुछ तकलीफें होती है ऐसी की इंसान खुद की नज़र में सिर भी ना उठा पाएगे और उन्ही में से कुछ तकलीफें देकर अपने खुद के किस्से सोकॉल्ड मर्दों को बताएगे... ये कैसा मनुष्य का व्यवहार है?

"Kuch" Kuch Dil Mein Baatein Chubh Hi Jaati Hai.

Kuch dil ke halat tham hi jaate hai ... Kuch umeedon kebaraat sapno mein hi reh se jaate hai... Kuch lafzon mein mehfooz khayaalat ban hi jaate hai... Kuch berukhi ke mausam panap se jaate hai... Kuch tammanaao ke aarzo dil mein utar se jaate hai... Kuch rooh mein basey cheharo ke shakal unke talwaar - i-jigar ko ghayal kar jaate hai... Kuch ibaadaton se rubaroo aur dilon ke chaahaton mein hoo -ba-hoo hone ke liye unka dilon ki dehleez par dustak dena chahtey hai...

Yeh Kaisi Bebasi Hai?

Yeh kaisi bebasi hai? Hum door hai phir bhi, humare beech mein religio n ki diwaare khadi hai... Yeh kaisi bebasi hai? Hum aaj pass hote hue bhi laakh kosh door hai, yeh dooriyon ne hi pairo mein jakad ke rakhi zanjeer hai .Yeh kaisi bebasi hai? Hum aaj khafa hote hue bhi tumhari baaton se itefaaq nahi rakh paa rahe hai, tum ho aisi Allah ki nayaab cheez, ki hum tumhein paaney ke liye khud se ladey jaa rahe hai... Yeh kaisi bebasi hai?

Dardon Ke Alag Hi Hisaab Hote Hai

Dardon ke alag hi hisaab hote hai, Kuch lafzon se toh kuch ghaaw ke nishaan se ban jaate hai. Yeh teri aashiqui se jaada khud meri yeh kaisi bebasi hai, Tu judaa ho chuka hai mujhse itni door ki meri aakhein aaj roro ke bheeg chuki hai... Dardon ke alag hi hisaab hote hai. Rishton ke hisaab naa titolu toh accha hai, tumse alag ho ke bhi khud ko doshi maanu sh ayad yahi mere gunaahon ki sazaa haiDardon ke alag hi hisaab hote hai.

"Tumse"

Tumse naa mil paaney ka dard yeh mere dil se poocho.Tumse naa aashiqui karne ki jurrat yeh mere zehan se poocho... Tumse kubool ki gayi minnaton ko un duaaon mein naa shaamil kiya ho toh poocho Tumse woh har baaton ka zikar NAA kiya ho toh poocho... Tumse har ek umeedon ki aash ko maine dilon ke taar se naa bandhaa ho poocho...

Priyanka K. Tiwari

Priyanka had a poetic disposition and a flair for writing from childhood on. Her first poem was published in a newspaper when she was 8. She has written many poems in English and Hindi, some of which appeared in local newspapers and magazines. To her, poetry is " Words that breathe, Emotions that bleed, Thoughts that burn!" A graduate in Biotechnology, she is currently associated with the field of HR - Organizational Psychology. Travelling, photography and reading are her passions.

She can be reached at -

Instagram: @pri_at_insta

and via email at words.verses.dreams@gmail.com

My Association With God

I have in Him, my guide and my friend,
His Love for me knows no definite end.

In Him, I find solace and peace,
My sufferings all, He did let cease

His Love is immortal, true and pure,
For my ailing heart, it's a real cure.

In Him, I seek the Divine Help,
Let my heart, no more, cry and yelp.

I've wandered enough in the quest of pleasure,
Found it neither in hustle nor in leisure.

Joy I find, in seeking refuge in Thee,
Who art the sole inspiration of me!

Let His Grace enlighten me and my deed,
My soul, let His immense Strength feed!

I cannot express, how great I feel,
When He fills me with love and zeal!

I offer my soul, heart and life to Him,
Who maketh my joys bright and sorrows dim!

I dedicate my little verse to His Name,
I seek Him; neither wealth nor fame!

One Autumnal Morn

The sky is clad in deep, damp shades,
Hanging mystically over the lonely glades.

Tints of scarlet, emerald, mauve and gold,
The overwhelming mystiques of the woods unfold.

Mist lies low over the craggy vales,
Rugged and beaten by the autumnal gales.

The multi-hued foliage, all dripping with pearly dew,
Drown the wooded landscape in a clear, transparent hue.

Blossoming luxuriantly the lilacs and daffodils
And daisies, carpet the distant rolling hills.

Silence and solitude wrap the wild, wild land,
Perfumed by the heady fragrance of the river sand.

Proud and majestic stand the lofty trees,
Swaying gracefully against the gentle breeze.

These still, serene woods in the hours small,
Abound in the sights and colors of the fall!

Hope

Hope is the soul of life
Hope is life's motivation
Follow your hopes with hope
And with the greatest dedication!

Let hopes grow within you
Into reality, let them bloom.
For even if they stay unreal
They still drive away gloom!

Lady Grace and Her Fantasy Land
(Recollection of a Dream)

I lay on my bed, so very cozy,
Full of ideas, all very rosy.

Boy oh! What happened in a trice!
There was I, amidst bird-cries.

In the Land of Perpetual Joy and Mirth,
Far, far away from the lonely earth.

In the fields of sparkling, golden wheat,
Dotted by shiny puddles, all so neat.

The soft breeze and the warm sun,
The meadows green; were all great fun!

Hark! Who is she, in a flowing gown?
Amidst the blossoms, in the valley down?

Lady Grace flashed a smile so warm,
It enhanced her bright, dazzling form.

She led me away with her hand,
To show the fantasies of Her Land.

The gently lapping sea and azure sky,
Stretched beyond the ken of the mortal eye.

We were greeted by the birds small,
Who charmed us with their little call?

There were fawns and squirrels shy

How with each other, they did vie!

And we came across a rainbow, so big,
As if the sky had donned a colorful wig.

She beckoned me to proceed and be bold
Which I did, and stumbled upon a pot of gold.

Lady Grace smiled, but her form became weak
Hey! Was that a slap I felt on my cheek?

I woke up confused, like a bird in a cage,
And faced two eyes, red with rage!

Its heart out, the alarm clock had cried,
Couldn't wake me up, how much it tried.

So, my mother lost all her cool
And tried to get me up for school.

But in my thoughts, still lives Lady Grace,
Stamped on my mind, is her charming face!

Re-Discovering Myself

I was hopelessly lost; meandering through the realms of dark,
When upon a new journey, I accidentally did embark...

That led to the discovery of my Self true;
All my limited self-conceptions, it did undo!

Erstwhile I had led a life not truly of my own,
Orchestrated by conditioning, my soul torn;

My Inner Light, eclipsed by my towering ego
Discernment clouded; couldn't tell a friend from a foe

Fragments of me, lost in gratification of senses
My inherent powers, diluted by petty indulgences

My mind, stuffed with what others fed...
Woe! Was it even my life that I led?

But today I am free, all by myself, alone,
My soul, my heart - for none but my own!

Shallow goals, my mind's long outgrown
A renewed dream, my eager hearts sown!

I have re-discovered my passions, ideals and aspirations,
Discarding my passivity, fears and self-imposed limitations!

I have a vision of my own to live by,
Let the world protest and ask why...

My potential, far exceeds what I had thought,
Only in my Higher Self, refuge I have sought!

Peace I have found, responding to my Higher Calling
I am defined by possibilities; not by any past failing!

To my inner Voice, I shall forever listen,
Under its aegis, I shall glow and glisten.

A rare Second Chance, I've been gifted by the Universe
To fully redeem MYSELF, battling circumstances all adverse!

Faith in my Own Self, and guided by the Divine Will
I renew my soul's mission – that greater Destiny to fulfill!

Riya Srivastava

Poet by passion and entrepreneur by action. My words to express my feelings and emotion to others connect with the hearts of many. Follow me on Instagram @riyashrivastava2000

Smile

A smile is a sign of love
A smile is a sign of care
A smile tells how much to others
You are important and also dear
A smile is a sign of cheer
A smile is a sign of trust
A smile shows how you can
Be happy even in hard crust
A smile is a sign of joy
A smile is a sign of hope
A smile teaches how you can
Remove the cloud of mope
For nothing but only a smile
Takes away your pain and trial
And pick you troubles pile
And let you smile and smile.

Never Give Up

It's madness.
To hate all roses
Because you got scratched by one thorn
To give up all your dream
Because one did not come true
To lose faith in prayers
Because one was not answered
To give up all your efforts
Because one of them failed
To condemn all your friends
Because one of them betrayed
Not to believe in love
Because someone was unfaithful
Remember that
Another chance may come up
Its new friend, it new love, its new life
Never give up on anything..............

आज की पीढ़ी

आज की पीढ़ी
माँ को पूछते हैं सभी
बाप को पूछते हैं सभी
काम पड़े तब तक रहे साथ
फिर बच्चे पूछे कौन हो आप।
अपना पेट काट कर जो
बच्चो के पूरे करते अरमान सभी
अपने फटे कपड़े पहनते
पर बच्चों को नई नई चीज़ दिलाते
हर गम हर दुख को पीकर
अपने बच्चों का भविष्य संवारते
बड़े होते ही बच्चे जिसे नही अपनाते
वही माँ बाप अपने बच्चों को हर दुख से बचाते
कर्तव्य हमारा है कि खयाल इनका रखना है
ये है तभी हमारे जीवन का चलना है।
भगवान से ऊपर जिनका दर्ज़ा होता है
उस माँ बाप का सारी दुनिया के दिलो पर कब्ज़ा होता है।

Bahan

Dil ka rishta hota h jisse,
Ek atut bharosa hota h jispe,
Ek dost,ek hamdard,ek sathi,
Jo hardam sath nibhati,
Jo ladti h jhagadti h par maanti h har kahna ,
Wo h meri pyari bahna,
Sath ghumna,masti karna,
Kabhi ek dusre ko chhedna,
To kabhi ek dusre ke liye khadi rahna,
Maa ke baad jo mamta ka ehsaas dilaye,
Wo hoti h bahna,
Ye rishta dil ka h jo kabhi tutata nahi,
Bahno ka pyar hi esa h jo kabhi chhutta nahi.

Maan ki Gehraiyo

Ek dariya jo gehraiyo se bhara,
Jisme pani nhi bahti h ansuo ki dhara,
Dariya tha man ka jisme gehraiyo badhti jati,
Aur in gehraiyo ko hm khud bhi n samjh pate,
Kahte h jab dard baya karo to man hlka ho jata h,
Par jab chot gehri ho to kuch kaha bhi ni jata h,
Samudra se bhi gehra hota h apna man,
N koi padh paya h n koi padh sakega,
In gehraiyo ko samjhne ke liye koi sachha dil milega,
Ye uthal puthal kb tk chalegi
Kab tak man me ek kasak si rahegi,
Shayad iska koi tod nhi.

Gumshuda

Talash h khud ki, n jane kaha gumshuda ho chuki hu,
Sabke sath to hu pr khud ko bhula chuki hu,
Bebas lachar nahi hu,
Bas duniya se anjaan ho chuki hu,
Majboot irade ab bhi h,
Bas mushkilo ne jhukna sikha diya,
Sabko majboot bnake khud ek unsuljhi raaz ban chuki hu,
Raah,chah,manzile,sab saath h,
Bas gumshuda h to zindagi ka wo pal,
Jise khushi banakar sab me baat diya,
Aur khud gumshuda kitaab ban chuki hu

Move On, Be Positive

Life laughs at you when you are unhappy,
Life smiles at you when you are happy,
But,
Life salutes you when you make others happy,
Throwback the shoulder let the heart sing,
Let the eyes flash,
Let the mind be lifted up,
Look upward the sky, and say to ourselves,
Nothing is impossible.

Baarish

Hazaaro bundo ki ek ladii,
Jamii pr aakr ro padi,
Achanak mitti ki nami me samakar,
Milan ki khushi me wo khil gyi,
Halki halki nami ke sath thande hawa ke jhoke,
Jaise koi prem geet ga rhe ho ek duje ka hoke,
Ek ek boond me h gajab ka saar,
Jo mazboot banate h do dilo ka pyar,
Boondo ki jhankar sangeet si mithi lagti h,
Jo mahsus krta h uske dil ko chhu jati h,
Ye mausam h dilo ko milane wala,
Jispe iski boonde pad jaati h,
Unki mohbbat khil jati h.

Arnab Dasgupta

Arnab Dasgupta, an MBA and an IT professional working for IT & ITES Sales and Account Management Team.
He is a person with varied emotions running in his heart and mind. His words can show what emotions he has. He   has a habit of penning down his thoughts, and currently discovering and exploring a hidden writer in himself. He has incorporated his study of spectrum of emotions in words. His writing and photography skills were published in several magazines, and he is also a co-author of several anthologies.
Hope you love the words and worlds.
Follow him on: Insta @imarnab_dg
Anyone can contact him on
arnab-dasgupta@hotmail.com

The Story of a Child from Sunset Hotspot

"With her blonde hair and striking hazel eyes, Adra cuts an elegant figure as she has launched her first documentary last month. Although the 27 -year-old lady seems a bit young to have completed a story about the life of people who are from sunset hotspots for men, and it's not an ordinary tale." The host of the felicitating ceremony was narrating the first line of his speech.

Adra sitting in the first row was deep in her thoughts, with a little smile on her face.

I am a journalist and an activist, but   not aligned with any organizations or groups. It was not my choice for not getting aligned to any news agency, but it was the society who dis   - owned me from mingling with them. What's the worst thing you could say about a person's mother? I grew up listening to all those words. "You are not our part; you are a by-product of a prostitute. You have mix -blood of 1000 fathers! Etc." How often I had heard those words? "You will not share in our inheritance," my room -mates in hostel used to tell me, and they forced me to leave the school even.

Today everyone is praising me just because I brought someone's life in day-light. Those lives that are not even considered as 'life', hence are not counted as a part of societal lives. Every strata of the people has the acce ss of these lives but only in the dark night. In the morning, they do not even want to step on their shadows. It is so ironic that in a society where dignified people use these women for recreation, the same society poses a threat to their identity itself.

With growing infrastructure, the corruption associated with it is also increases, but sadly the government chooses to just look at the sun to avoid the shadows. They might have evolved into best animals on the earth, but 'Wild' is still their nature. People say- "This is not my responsibility. The government officials and police is to be blamed." Maybe because they are afraid of taking Responsibility. I took the responsibility, if not for my nation I live in, and not for the world I breathe, at least for Humanity.

"But with extraordinary strength and determination, at the age of 27, she managed to pull herself out of the groove, beat her ill-addictions and go to institutions where she obtained her degrees and totally turned her life around." The host was continuing with his speech. These sentences disrupted her thoughts, and brought her back to present.

She looked at the host who was busy with his speech. She looked at her watch, 15 more minutes' post which the documentary will be on-screen. Fortunately, I succeed in making this documentary and got raving reviews on You Tube and other social media platform.

When I thought of making a documentary on them, I did not receive a single support from anyone be it from any so -called respected individuals or from some so -called rights saving organizations. Everyone not only made a mockery of my project, they also did their best for my project's failure.

By the grace of Almighty, I was able to complete my project and I was felicitated by several international organizations. After my name spread beyond boundaries, my own motherland looked at me. She realized that even those lives are part of their own soil, they are her daughters but are not given their due respect.

Today, our state government has felicitated me, and the 90 minutes documentary will be shown on a big display in next few minutes.

"Now, I would request Adra to come on the podium and start the documentary along with our Information and Broadcasting Minister." The host gave his final statement, and there was a huge round of applause.

Adra rose from her seat, went towards the podium. She went to her knees, and touched her forehead on the steps of the dais. She stepped up. The minister felicitated her with a shawl and a memento, a souvenir for her spirit. She was asked to share few words.

The sound of claps was hammering the ear -drum. With loads of tears in h er eyes, she went towards the microphone. The clapping was stopped by now. "Thank you everyone for making themselves available in the midst of their busy schedule. Thank you every one for making a creature like me feel good. I have nothing much to say. I a m overwhelmed. Would request the team to proceed with the documentary." She said with a heavy voice.

She came back to her seat. Gradually lights were turned off, and the dark auditorium was filled with white lights coming from big screen.

The story begins with a narration.

The word 'tawaif' is a word rich with emotional connotations. The term 'tawaif' is the plural form of the Arabic 'Taifa', and as such meant group. Later the term has become synonymous with a prostitute. However, Mirza Jafar Husain, w ho spent most of his life in the traditional atmosphere of twentieth   -

century Awadh society, observed that the word tawaif baazi for whoring was never used in Lucknow. The equivalent word "r@*** baazi" for whore-mongers was considered to be vulgar. In better society, the expressions employed were tamash bini, which means libertinism or licentiousness, and aiyyashi, or debauchery.

Such was the fascination associated with it, and desire for courtesans in Lucknow that the nineteenth -century rekhtigo poet Mirza Ali Baig 'Nazneen' Dehalvi wrote:

Kya jaaniye kya kasbiyon mein shahad ghula hai
Ghar walion se khush koi shauhar nahin hota

(One does not know what honey pot the prostitutes have. No husband seems happy with his own wife)

"Yet, there was a time when tawaifs were treated as the epitome of etiquette and culture. They were the preservers of north Indian music and dance, and hobnobbed with the nobility," says Chote Miyan, heir to a kotha in Chowk, the old market of nawabi Lucknow.

In the 1980s, when the kotha culture was on the decline, a girl named Romila grew up in one of the major sunset hotspots for men who wanted to shower notes on the singing-dancing nautch girls, or courtesans. She would hear someone shouting out 'daughter of a bi***' to shame her. Her mother was sold in a major market much before she attained puberty.

For Romila, her mother's profession was like a magician's bravura performance. She used to gaze her mother like she is a real princess as she wore stunning costumes, and she smelled of exotic perfumes. She danced like an acrobat. She used to

watch her in awe and imbibed some of her steadfast qualities, though she can hardly match her footwork, or her vocal pitch.

Unknown about the reality of the profession her mother was in, she wanted to be like her mother. One day she asked her mother, "Mamma, you look so stunning. Neither of these aunties are as beautiful and gorgeous as you are. I want to be like you, and I will look as stunning as you." Her mother when realized wanted to keep her away from these darkened part of the society.

What was difficult to deal is not t he job but the complexities of adjusting to the worlds inside and outside the arena. Inside the arena, life was heaven, however outside, hell awaits. Using her contacts from her permanent patrons, her mother enrolled Romila in a nearby convent school so th at she does not need to face the rotten section of society, but even in that so -called disciplined and sophisticated school she was subjected to harassment. She was being harassed by the boys on the playground. They were offering her bucks for a feel, whic   h was not within her understanding at that age.

The boys used to touch her sometimes, few of them used to put money in her pocket in lieu of those coercive touch and feel. As those were not within her understanding, she used to sob in the dark. When the m   other came to know about the same, she was forced to make a difficult decision. As she was unable to protect her daughter from the level of stigma and discrimination she was experiencing in school, she moved her daughter to a far boarding school.

She changed her name from Romila to Tara, change her city as well. However, fate travels with people. The past harassment used to haunt her in dreams. After few months, even in the new school she has to face the same harassment,

and have to stay all alone. The att ention Tara received from teachers and officials ostensibly concerned for her well-being was overwhelmingly negative. It took her some time getting used to the taunts she was subjected to. Course books, and other study materials helped her to cope with the ignominy she faced every day. She immersed herself in studies, became an autodidact chewing up the school library, and burnished the ambition to become an orator, and a social activist from an early age. She did not have this inclination or intelligence because she wanted to tell her mother's story.

Over the years, the cuss words r**** ki beti, daughter of a b**** became ineffective. Education has fortified her to disregard humiliation. Abuse no longer rankled her.

She passed all her exams in flying colors, got scholarships for her higher studies in abroad. She completed her higher studies, and at the same time she worked for her dreams. She also completed journalism and joined social activists' group that works for the upliftment of the non -existence citizens of the country for gathering know-how of their daily work.

When Tara a.k.a Romila returned to her motherland, she was offered a 'Chief Editor' position in one of the leading news channels.

But, by the time she went back to the place of her origin, her mother's soul has already left this world. The government arrested few from the group, destroyed several houses, and victimized many, as they considered it to be a rotten part of the society. The minsters who used to visit this place in the mid of the night passed an order to demolish the locality or keep them out of society; The police who used to take daily, weekly, or monthly sweetener from the locality started following the

order to ruin the area. The women who were arrested were tortured and raped behind the bars.

She accepted the offer from the leading news channel, and used it as a medium for the upliftment of those who are considered as non-existing creature in day-light. After 15 years, she is running a successful organization that helps the offspring of the lady staying in sunset hotspots to grow and live a respectable life. For Tara, balancing motherhood and journalism work is not just about sneaking around. Doing journalism for ten years, sometimes on the street, actually helped prepare her for motherhood. "The ability to read a dangerous situation, stay calm, not show your reactions, is a very important skill," she points out. "If I'm worried about something, I can talk to my mates without being verbally aggressive."

The lights were turnedon, everyone was sitting speechless and motionless with tears in their eyes.

Barsha Das

In the kingdom of writing her words are loyal to poetry and in the world of people she holds a medical degree. In both ways she saves lives.

You can find her at Instagram @ drbarsha16 and @ shower_of_thoughts

The Dough of Life

Fallen leaves
never grow again
but they get to kiss the earth

we find a new shelter
when we leave the old one,
"life is like that!"

the tree weeps
for each of its leaf
but continues to grow
though it seems hard

we let go of things
that hurt
and move on
"growing up is like that"

The Ocean Love Bakery

Drop by drop
I squeezed myself
from the ocean of love

little by little
I poured myself
In dried hopes to refill

day by day
I raised myself
to make my own way

step by step
I am moving myself
to build another ocean without any help

Call Me A Pie: The Stuffing Inside Are Heavenly!

It's not easy to fly
under water
but I learnt

It's not easy to play
with fire
yet I burnt

It's not easy to walk
barefoot
but I walked

It's not easy to fathom
every storm
yet I engulfed

I endured everything
that I fear and despise
yet I laughed!

Cookies Aren't Always Soft

Everyone wants rose petals,
no one asks for the cactus
but you know what!
I will never leave your side
even when you are all dried up

Petals are soft and scented
but they wilt and wither
in the cold snowy winter
and in a hot sweaty summer

Cactus adds green to your fields
though it's prickly and rough,
in the rains
and in summer it stands by you
making alive your hope

Life is a hard journey so is love
it's not about being hard or soft
but to stand by thick and thin
and when you find someone like that
 you know that's enough

The Leftover Cake

When I walk through the woods
behind me,
I hear your footsteps

When I sit by the river
I hear your heart beats
Like my head resting on your chest

When I lie under the starry night
I hear your whispers
louder than the chirps of crickets

I can hear you everywhere
No matter how hard I try, not to
even years after you left

The Burnt Brownies

Under the clouds
weeps the sun
under the pillow
my complicated emotion

Beneath the surface
burns the earth
beneath my chest
a broken heart

Behind the curves of earth
struggles the crescent moon
behind the curtains of society
my voiceless tune

In the deep silence
dies the darkest night

Rudra Gupta

A name is a worth of thousand conversation. Rudra Gupta is from UP (bijnor). She started writing a few month   ago. She like arts and crafts She is a creative person and like doing things with her hands. She uses a creative approach to solve her problem. She is always energetic and eager to learn new skills.

खुशियों की चाबी

आयी थी खुशियों की चाबी,
 नयी मुस्कान के साथ।
जब जन्मी थी बिटिया प्यारी,
नन्ही किलकारी के साथ।

सुबह की ख़ुशी भी वही थी,
शाम की पहर भी वही थी।
मेरी एक मुस्कान थी जिसमे,
खुशियों से भरा संसार भी वही थी।

सबको मिलकर खूब हँसाती,
सबसे अपने लाड लडवाती।
कभी यहाँ से कभी वहाँ से,
एक प्यारी सी मुस्कान दे जाती।

नन्हें-नन्हें पाँव लेकर आयी थी
खुशियों की चाबी बनकर,
मन को हमारे गुदगुदाती थी,
प्यार का एक प्यारा सा एहसास कराती थी।

आयी थी वो खुशियों की चाबी,
जैसे हमारे घर को महकाने,
अब बड़ी होकर चली है,
वो नया संसार बसाने।

दायरा लड़की का

शुरू हुई हस्ती खेलती ज़िंदगी मेरी
फिर एक मोड़ पर आकर यू रुक सी गयी
लड़की हो कहकर जब बेड़ियाँ मेरे कस दी गयी
इस समाज को मेरा कदम ना भाया
कभी रंग रूप तो कभी पहनावा बोल रुकवाया
हर शकस यहाँ मुझको मेरा दायरा समझाता है
लड़की हो बोलकर मेरा हर काम रुकवाता है
थे मेरे भी सपने कुछ बन दिखाने के
पर थे समाज के भी सपने लड़की को घर में घुसाने के
परायी अमानत को तो एक दिन पराए घर ही जाना था
इस घर से उसका दाना पानी उठ जाना था
लड़की नही बहूँ हो यह ताना उसको वहाँ दे दिया जाता था
बहूँ हो कहकर फिर दायरा समझाया जाता था
कहने को लड़के के बराबर होती है लड़कियाँ
फिर क्यूँ लड़की हो कहकर दायरा समझाया जाता था
कुछ सवाल है अपनो से कुछ समाज से पूछना है मेरा
एक लड़की हूँ इसलिए क्यूँ है एक दायरा मेरा

बातें कलम से

मेरी कलम आज कल कुछ भी लिख जाती है
सच मेंथोड़ा ज़्यादा चलती झूट मेंपीछे हट जाती है
जो बातें मैं कभी कह नही पाती हूँ
आज कल वो सब कलम कह जाती है
बिलखती हुई लड़कियों की दास्तान लिखती कभी
तो कभी रेप का दर्द लिख जाती है
माँ की ख़ुशी का एहसास लिखती कभी
तो कभी ससुराल के दर्द लिख जाती है
लिखती हूँ दर्द कभी इतने की कलम भी रो उठती है
खुद तो है गमगींन मुझे क्यू तू रुलाती है
क्यू दर्द दुनिया के सारे मुझसे ही लिखवाती है
चल कलम वादा कर राज को राज रखेगी
तो मैं बात तेरी भी मान लेती हूँ
आज तेरी स्याही में डूबकर कुछ ख़ुशनुमा पल लिख जाती हूँ
होता है एहसास ख़ुशी का
जब बात तुझसे होती है
रोता है मन्न मेरा जब याद तेरी आती है
तेरी एक पुकार ही इन होठों पर हंसी दे जाती है
वो तेरी तीखी नज़र प्यार का एहसास कराती है
होता है असमंजस मुझको
तेरे यू बिन बोले समझ लेने पर
तो मिलती है ख़ुशी भी बहुत
इस अनजाने से एहसास से
तेरा बोलना" तू रोया ना कर जान निकल जाती है "
कितनी बार रोते रोते मुझको यह बात चुप करा जाती है
और एक धीमी से मुस्कान मुँह पर दे जाती है
चल आज तेरी मेरी बातों को कुंछ ऐसे याद करते है
बस हम तो यू ही ख़ुशियों का एहसास करते है

पढ़कर ये बातें कलम भी मुस्कुराने लगी
उसको कब कैसे तू इतना चाहने लगी
चाह तो बहुत है बस तुझको आज बताया है
राज को राज ही रखने का वादा जो तुझसे कराया है

दिल की मैं अपनी हसरत लिख रही हूं।

तुझसे हुई शिद्दत से मोहब्बत लिख रही हूं।। जिसे मैं कर न सकी कभी लब से बयां। कलम से मैं अपनी वो तेरी चाहत लिख रही हूं।। मिलता है सुकून जो तेरे से बात कर के। आज दिल को मिली वो राहत लिख रही हूं।। बातों ही बातों से ले लेते है जो सुकून हम तुम शब्दों में समेट कर हमारी वो यादें लिख रही हूं।। लिखने को तो लिख दूं हर एहसास को मैं। पर तेरी ना छूटने वाली अपनी वो आदत लिख रही हूं।। रहो तुम जहां कही भी ओ मेरे हमदम। तेरी खुशी से जुड़ी रहे हर कड़ी तुम्हारी यही अरदास लिख रही हूं।। दूरियों में भी होने वाली वो परवाह लिख रही हूँ दर्द मालूम होते हुए भी आह ना करने वाला वो एहसास लिख रही हूँ हर पल का किया हुआ वो तेरा इंतज़ार लिखा रही हूँ कितना करती हूँ आज भी तुझसे प्यार लिख रही हूँ कभी ना होने वाला दीदार लिख रही हूँ विडीओ कॉल पर ही बात वाली ख़ुशी का एहसास लिख रही हूँ हुमाइ वफ़ा की कहानी लिख रही हूँ एक दूसरे के प्यार का एहसास लिख रही हूँ ।। रिश्ते में पार किए हुए पड़ाव लिख रही हूँ फिर भी समझौता हालात ना करने वाले बुलंद इरादे लिख रही हूँ थोड़ा प्यार लिख रही हूँ

(5)

एक अजीब सी ज़िंदगी बक्शी है ख़ुदा ने भी की एक अजीब सी ज़िंदगी बक्शी है ख़ुदा ने भी हमको इंसान बनाकर एक इनायत बरसी है ख़ुदा ने भी ग़म और ख़ुशी दो पहलू बने है ज़िंदगी के भी की ग़म और ख़ुशी दो पहलू बने है ज़िंदगी के भी किसी के पास सब ख़ुशी होकर भी वो ग़म में है तो कोई ग़म पाकर भी यहाँ ख़ुश सा है   एक सफ़र सी बनी है ज़िंदगी हमारी कुछ यार मिले तो मिले कुछ दुश्मन कुछ चोट मिली तो मिले कुछ मरहम कुछ यादें मिली तो मिले कुछ आंसू कुछ अपने मिले तो मिले कुछ पराए अब बचपन छूटा थोड़ी जवानी आयी थोड़ी हमको निभानी दुनिया दारी आयी छूटा जब कुछ अपनो का साथ तो पता चला यही तो असली जिंदगनी आयी आते है नित नए रंग ज़िंदगी में कुछ खुलके हँसाते है तो कुछ बहुत रुलाते है कुछ पल नए रिश्ते दे जाते है तो कुछ पल बने बनाए रिश्ते भी तोड़ जाते है बस यही तो ज़िंदगी है जहां कब क्या हो जाए कुछ पता नहि लगती बस ख़ुदा की बक्शी एक इनायत सी है ज़िंदगी

माँ

एक ऐसा शब्द जिसको परमात्मा से ऊँचा दर्जा दिया जाता है पर कभी सोचा है की ऐसा क्यू है माँ क्या है हमारे लिए ?माँ शब्द ही प्यार का सबसे बड़ा एहसास है हमारी चोटी सी हँसी पर अपने सब दुःख भूल जाती है माँ हमारे एक आँसू से सहम सी जाती है माँ दुख हमको होता है आँखें माँ की रोती है ख़ुश हम होते है मुस्कान उसके लबों पर होती है बच्चों के मच्छर भी काटे तो दवाई बोलकर क्रीम लगती है खुद का हाथ भी कट जाए तो दो दिन बाद बोलती है य कब कट गया पता ही नहि चला ऐसी होती है माँ मां बीना जिंदगी वीरान सी होती है अंधियारी रातों में थपकी देकर कभी सुलाती है माँ खुद रात भर जागती पर एहसास तक ना दिलाती माँ कभी प्यार से चूमती है तो कभी डाँटकर पास बुलाती है माँ आए कभी आँख में आंसू तो तुरंत आँचल से पूछती है माँ सपनों के झूलों में अक्सर धीरे-धीरे हमको झुलाती है माँ सब दुनिया से रूठ रपटकर जब मैं बेमन से सो जाती हूँ तो हौले से अपने सीने मुझे लगाती है माँ हर सुख दुःख की खबर रखती है माँ बिन बोले ही सब कुछ समझ जाती है माँ इतना सब कुछ करके भी कभी कभी प्यार के दो बोल को तरस जाती है माँ पर कभी ना शिकायत करती माँ

Roopali Purohit

Roopali is a hopeful optimistic and full of life person she loves reading stories and weaving them in her head and putting them on paper.

(1)

Dear someone special,

I always opt for the sentence that I miss you but there are emotions that swirl within my heart thataches for you missing you is a mere sentence,
and you know why my heart aches for you?
I will answer you because you don't want me to have an iota of change in me, you never diminish me and my ideas, you love the way I held myself with confidence.
You support me but do not suffocate me and I know the difference.
Even if we have to say goodbye the respect, we have for each other will always be there and when I will have to leave you a part of me will die because that part will always ache to have you by my side.

(2)

So, we all know the story of a hen who gave a golden egg daily and since childhood we have been taught that story the message delivered being greedy is bad, but we forgot to focus on one thing that this normalized.

The fact that killing of hen was wrong, taki ng a golden egg and getting benefit from it daily was the whole purpose.

Now all of us have figured this story by now but now it's a trend that let's normalize being greedy, let's forget the story but when did that story conveyed that getting the egg was wrong, similarly milking your talent, working hard in what you believe in, investing properly and growing day by day should be a daily practice.

What should not be the daily practice is to kill the hen, every hen who have the magical golden egg because once   all these magical hens will be slaughtered, we will be resource less and helpless.

Also, one more thing we forget to learn is that impatience and hasty decisions always leads to a path of destruction and the last thing and the most important thing that it   teaches is that such magical things should be given to the people who have skills, ambitions, patience, hard work and intelligence without all this the hen will either end up killed or the person who possesses that kind of hen will be butchered so next time let's read stories again and learn more from them

(3)

Dear belief,
I had you in my adolescence like a heavy bag of jewels.
One day your burden became too heavy, the strain making me too weary
So, I lost you in the sea of maturity, bit by bit every day.
Without the light of you the sea of maturity was dark and I was floating without any guidance.
At the end by sheer luck, I found a piece of you and now in the sea of maturity I am trying get that bag again so heavy and letting myself weary.

(4)

Euphoria I was intoxicated by you, but never dared to say it on your face. Your aura so intimidating that I stayed away, but I saw you looking back at me and you promised me to take me with you on a ride. A ride which so rough that I won't be able to reach the touch of my sanity and I lived in the euphoria of that promise which you delivered.

(5)

I crave happily ever after; I wait for the perfect person to hold my eye. I swipe left and right hoping to reach someone to catch more than what's just beyond the sparkling   light. I sigh with disappointment when I get liked for my skin, I sigh with anger when every guy who catches m y eye says I am fire and they don't want to get burn. And I wonder when will I get my own sky where I shine whole life. I crave happily ever after, but as soon as I get closer, i realize not everyone is a sky and i sigh again with hope and disappointment.   As they say it sees the right eye to find the jewel inside the dye.So, with a sigh I wait for someone to stay after knowing my value and who does not get the high and low after seeing the sunshine. It's not my fault that I haven't catches the guy with a right eye. So, I wait again.

(6)

Duty of every human towards their   body, when it's at the epitome of its   beauty When   hairs and skin are healthy the beauty glows from inside but at21, We forget that duty, eating staying unfit became the beauty of life. And our body refuses to cope taking a toll to remind us our   duty, the reminders are horrible, blemishes on skin, constant diseases it became the reality and we are reminded of our   duty. After receiving the message from our body, we remember our duty and learn the importance of duty to give our body the real beauty that is of a healthy lifestyle as our bodies are the gift of almighty and it is our duty to cherish every gift including our body.

Rutba Qayoom

Meet her, she is Rutba Qayoom resident of Kashmir, currently pursuing law degree from University of Kashmir. She is very passionate about writing and has complied almost 600 quotes, poems and short essays at the age of 21. She has also worked as a Coaut hor in couple of anthologies. She preferably writes on social issues, motivational thoughts etc.

Topaz in Crown

Lit the candles of success.
Let yourself grow and shine.
Extinguish old lamps of despair.
Be your own scholar and princess.
Inhale positive thoughts and forget the pain.
Elevate your status by recalling lessons you gain.
Be crazy for your dreams and aims.
Be your own brand and exclaim.
Vandalise your enemies and worries.
Shine like a topaz in crown.
Be the changing figure of the town.
Act wisely and fill your heart with merries.
Courage, faith and perseverance should be rules.
Be patient, rarest one takes time to bloom.

Advice to Learners

Unfortunately, on the advent of examination in any field, we
as learners become tense, confused and disturbed. We fall into
a dilemma what, how and when to do anything.
My dear learner keep calm and realize that a single test doesn't
determine your intell ect and worth. Neither bundle of marks
nor paper full of errors could destroy your image. We all are
learners here, take it at ease and don't hurt your self-esteem.
Real exams are yet to come in our lives as we grow in the shape
of miseries and difficulties, learn how to justly deal with them.

Listen Patiently

Don't judge someone on the basis of who he/ she was yesterday or long before because every new sunrise changes a person completely either positively or negatively. Yesterday's saint may turn into heinous criminal or vice versa. Human is full of errors; every saint has a past and every sinner has a future. So, behave and decide patiently.
Remember,
No one is saint here; everyone has sinned in one form or other.

Talk about Parents

Parent symbolizes union and amalgamation of different emotions into single soul. We can say angelic souls. Unfortunately, in today's busy and modern world, we usually feel shy and Awkward when time comes to their introduction. Those who have sacrificed the ir lives just to make you feel special and comfortable. Those whose hands turned rough and pale, wrinkled face, now bothers us. Try to appreciate and spend quality time with them, you don't know when death knocks at the door. "Start from now" should be you   r next thought. My dear readers, sometimes conflicts may and will arise between you and your parents but neither you will be wrong nor they, it's just generation gap. Try to ignore these stupid trifles. Make sure to hug your parents at least once in a day as a mark of respect.

(5)

To reach heights cultivate humanity in yourself. When you become sober, caring and understanding definitely all the treasures of world will pay homage to you. Reaching heights is not always about materialistic and professional achievement, sometimes it's just to elevate in your own eyes and conscience.

(6)

To heal your wounds completely, sometimes you have to accept some bitter truths. There is no alternative to it. Ignoring and disconnection makes it even worse. To heal yourself completely you have to let them go and let yourself grow. During this process don't forget to make yourself believe that whatever happens has a reason behind, it was just an experience to make you more sober and strong. Face hardships of life with smiling face, "Despite   burning, roses smell awesome aroma" should be the catchy line of your healing process. Above all, spend quality time with yourself and with those who are in need of a shoulder to cry and confidant listener. Heal the wounds of others your own will stop bleeding.

Anwesa Chakraborty

She is Anwesa Chakraborty, pursuing VFX (Visual Effects) from Hi-Tech Animation, Shyambazar, lives in Kolkata, West Bengal, India. Completed her Graduation, from University of Calcutta in 2019, after that she started writing. Also, a photographer, but not professional, because she loves to capture what she likes and finds interesting, nature soothes her, and greenery gives her peace. Thus, most of her writings and poems are based on nature, uses very simple language that everyone can understand. She has been a part of some Anthologies named L'amour in 2020 and Confession Beyond Curtain, Khubsurat Safar, MomMy world, Tranquility, Life goes on! in 2021. Her writing has a touch of abstract feature, which is appreciated by all. You can find her writings and connect with her on Instagram - @the_parrot_says,
E-mail - chakrabortyanwesa@gmail.com .

The Photographer

A child caged in the four walls, only questioned why nature is so beautiful and why can't we see it every time!! He used to take the scattered crayons on the ground and paint them on the white walls but was never satisfied. His siblings always asked him to come out and play with them, but a question that he always asked was "can you give me a rainy view in summer?" whose answer they did not know, thus again left ca   ged. His thoughts and visualization were bounded and trapped inside the four walls, thus some of them said he became mentally disabled. Thus, the parents thought to admit him to the hospital for his treatment.

He slept with the reflection of the moonligh at night. He gazed at his hands and saw the shine of the light after some time ambulance came and without any notice to the boy they took him. He was not in his sense when he walked down the staircase. As he went inside the ambulance, he asked the staff, whether they are going to see rain in this heat. The staff gave a sarcastic smile and said "NO". He said "ok". But, his reply had full of emotions rather than a casualty. His parents did not say a word when the staff took their child. He was happy by traveling through the roads, he smiled, as he never saw such colors. The midnight lights were a joyous moment for him. He was 8 years old. Soon they reached the hospital. He smiled on his own as if he could visualize those light trails when he walked through t he corridor. Other patients teased him and gave sarcastic smiles which he ignored. As he was a child, was kept in that ward. that night he did not sleep rather only gazed at the moon and the lights inside the room.

In the morning the doctor visited each   ward and when the doctor visited him, again he asked the same question "can you give me a rainy view in summer?" But the doctor did not smile

nor spoke a word just went away prescribing him a diet chart but did not give any medicine. All the kids went outs ide to play. He also went out, but as he was caged into four walls, he was unable to bear the natural light, thus he behaved differently and again taken to the four-walled room. He never went out of the four walls, into the vast nature amidst the natural lights, nor those waterfalls, winds, and the earthy smell. The doctor who visited him saw his behavior and suddenly he bought crayons, a board, a sheet and asked the child to draw what he sees or what he visualizes.

The child was more than happy. He snatc hed the crayons and sheets and started to draw. He was not satisfied by the first drawing, so he had torn out the sheet into pieces and was going to paint on the walls, soon the doctor approached him and provided him more sheets to draw on it. The doctor t ook a close view of his behavior and provided sheets after sheets. Soon the ward was messy with torn papers. The doctor went and asked the nurses to give filling food but no medicines.

The next day he tried to get out of his ward and see the natural light but again he behaved differently. The doctor kept the sheets last night on his table, and he again started painting. But today also he was not satisfied with his painting, but he did not tear it, rather kept it as it is on his bed. He went to the corridor was searching for the doctor, and he had a sharp memory. As he walked through the corridor, he forwarded his hand to the sunlight and gazed at it as if he held the sun in his hand. The glow of the sun attracted him, and again he tried to go out into the natural light, but this time without thinking of his difficulty he went out, he could not bear the strong light but his willpower made him do so. Soon he fainted, the nurses hurried and took him to the ward and called the doctor, and immediately his treatment was done but did not give any medicine, only glucose water. Soon the doctor asked the nurses to shift him to a cabin, where he would stay alone. The staff could not understand why the doctor asked them to do so! During lunchtime, he was shifted to a pe   rsonal cabin from where he could see nature. He showed the drawing as soon as the doctor visited him. He said the doctor that he did not like his painting, but wanted to show him. The doctor asked the reason for the same, he answered that, what he visualiz es, he can't bring out exact colors thus comes up with different colors, that he can't see in that natural light especially in the morning. After looking at his painting, the doctor said, he would be a "photographer". The child was stunned by the word "PHOTOGRAPHER", and without knowing anything about it, he said, "I want to learn this art", and the doctor left. The whole day he only painted different views on the pieces of paper. After a week his parents came to see him, as the doctor called them. The chil d was stable and did not undergo any mental disability, so they can take him home. But the child refused as he knew that again he would be caged. The parents also refused to take him, as they were more concerned about society than their child. And for thisreason, the doctor took all the responsibility of the child, and the child was taken by the doctor to his house, located amidst natural bliss.

After two days the doctor took the child to his house. As if the child's journey for becoming a photographer h ad started. The child got admission to a good school, and also the doctor every day showed him different photographs and also the color tones they use. Gradually he started his education and grew elder over time and his behavior also changed. Now he does not fear the natural light, rather whenever he gets time starts painting on canvas in the backyard of the doctor's house. After completing his school life the doctor did not force him to study the stereotype education but always supported him to study what he wanted. But he thought it to an end because the doctor was severely injured due to an accident. The money which the

doctor earned was not sufficient to buy a camera for him, and he felt guilty and thought himself to be an uninvited guest. The doctor did not have a family, thus considered him to be his son. As the doctor wanted him to see as a photographer, he asked him to sell his paintings to the public, and he did so. Soon he arranged a good amount of money. His paintings had so much color play that he was paid more than the actual price of the painting. With this money and some of the doctor's money, he managed to get a chance in one of the photography schools, for learning the art as he said earlier. But this art needs a device too, but he did not h ave that much money to buy a camera. Sometimes he borrowed from people and sometimes got it by paying rent. Soon this was also coming to an end, as he could not clear the photography school's fees, he was rusticated. But as we know if we put forward our go od gestures, it returns to us in a lucrative way. And by this, he met a stranger who was like God's messenger to him. The stranger used to keep an eye on him, his drawings, and his photography as a beginner. The stranger offered Clarke a chance to learn ph   otography with him without any allowance, but in return, he just asked him to click such pictures which would be different from the crowd. He agreed to it and his journey started to become a photographer.

He clicked random pictures of people, street, and   others, but nothing could satisfy the stranger and for that, he was kept outside the stranger's house for months. And one day he captured a bird's photograph and shown to him, which attracted his eyes, and soon was placed inside the house. Season changed, the weather changed, and Clarke also grew elder. Now, he travels to different places and captures beautiful moments, and also became a well-known photographer. And his quest for getting 'a rainy view in this heat' was also fulfilled, and he realized that a photographer can capture those live moments and cherish them in any season.

He was also awarded BEST PHOTOGRAPHER of the year. The photograph was of the doctor and the stranger, but he could not cherish that happy moment with them, as they died when he was in quest of getting a rainy view in the heat.

Now he owns a DSLR camera, a house that is full of colors, decorated with his captured pictures, name, and fame, and also a teacher at his photography school.

The eight-year-old child (Clarke), who was caged in four walls, now became a famous photographer and his quest for a rainy view in summer also fulfilled, and the doctor's belief was also fulfilled but his journey for off-track photography is still alive.

Gayatri Sharma

Dear readers she is Gayatri Sharma from   Malkangiri district of Odisha. She is continuing her graduation in BSc. Writing is not only a passion for her but also a different way to live her life. According to her she writes nothing but her own feelings, own experiences and puts her own soul on the paper. She never let her dreams to be deleted from her mind. She captures and writes them on the papers. Her father Mr.Supriya Kumar Nath is her inspiration . She is a conscious dreamer. Hope!! You are gonna love the poetry.

Present in Past

1.I was sitting near the sea floor
listening the music of evening
while the twilight sun
busy in kissing the agile waves
i was smoking
the tears deep inside my lungs
In between the,
chilly winds and floating clouds...
 I was trying to be present
at the moment with the rover sands
On that eventless evening
with false hope of perfection
and mystical decoction of prosperity
I was demanding,
to be alive,
Within the pages of poetry.

History

we were there before the history,
we will be there after the future,
Someone started the story
someone ended it
But the story itself,
Neither has an introduction nor the conclusion
Behind every silence
There is a screaming history
Behind every lost moon
There is a dark night.
some blind eyes busy in
looking at the darkness of night
some athirst eyes love busy in
searching the moon behind the clouds
But the night itself is a history and myth of our heart.

A Letter of Truth

In the envelope of lies
Having the smiling tears.
A numb spirit in a moving body
A question mark entangled in every relation
A dead soul in a living body
Repeatedly dealing with,
the word reconciliation ...
An untold story with hunting memories.
A sleeping bird hidden behind,
These shinning eyes.
A lost key of a closed room.
A cheerful breeze with moisture.
Where everything ends, they begin.
With their pen, paper and sleepless nights.

I Am Lost

A lot to say, A lot to write
But I have a limit to cry.
I am lost, an ever-wandering soul,
Searching for the lost piece,
Of the puzzle of my life
I am oblivious to the truth,
I am an illusion to my own story.
Rummaging in a library,
to know the eternal truth
I am the unsung Lyrics,
I am the faded reality
waiting for the divine intervention,
Just to write my destiny,
On the paper of Justice.

जिंदगी

बीते हुए कल से सीकायत,
आने वाले कल पे सवाल...
खानाबदोशी में गुजरती हुई रूह,
और जवाब के तलाश में ठहरी हुई जिस्म।
बिन पंखों के परिंदा,
फलक तक उड़ जाने की खवाबिंदा .
टूटी हुई ख्वाब बिखरा हुआ वक़्त है,
ठिकाना एक ही था,मंज़िल भी एक ही है..
बस राह मुसाफिरों का अलग है,
और जिंदेगी इसिका नाम है...

She Is A Writer

Lost between billions of wonders
Feels the taste of adversity
while welcoming all the prosperity.
Yes! She is a writer ...

Never let her dreams to be deleted
from her mind
She put down the blues in the whites
she feels the love, she feels the pain.
she is empathetic, she is sympathetic
yes! She is a Writer

In the Spells of nature and musical evening
In the rains, in the rainbows
From the hell to heaven.
Starting from the drop of ink
to her destination.
She writes the untold literature
yes! she is a writer.

Twin Flame

Hold him today,
Hug him so tight,
Even the wind can't pass between you
Look at his eyes today,
Those eyes with secret desires
Make those secrets to be written in thy stories.
Hold his head close to your heart,
let him listen your heartbeat,
that is beating only for him...
let him listen your untold word,
put his hand in yours,
Make him understand he is not alone,
He is just in a twin flame journey
Moving towards his destiny with you

Beautiful She

Her heart speaks clear and loudly
she quite her mind
and float like a cloud

Her eyes are musical like sunset
waiting for the singing Waves
on the sea floor, to make her naked soul wet.

Her lips are still and silent
Rhyming her smiles
while receiving the blessings from universe
to give her back a pile

वाकिफ

यूं मौसम के बाद मौसम बदलते रहे,
कुछ देर साथ चले थे ,और रास्ता बदल गए।

शीशे की ख्वाब लेकर चले थे सायद,
की अंधेरों से मुलाक़ात हुई ,फिर सारे टूट गए।

वो चांद भी रोज ढूंढती थी मुझे ज़मीन पर,
जब हम हाथ बढ़ाए तो ,फिर बादलों में कहीं खो गए।

वो भी कुछ इस तरह वाकिफ थे इस इश्क़ की दस्तूर से,
में उनसे इजहार करू इससे पहले ही वो इनकार कर गए।

Sayandeep Patra

A boy from a small town always had a dream of becoming a writer is heading towards to fulfill the dream.

(1)

Kuch muskan o ka koi kimat nahi hota,
Jaise chai ko cheene ke alawa koi swad nahi ata.

(2)

Zindagi mein jeene ke do e tarike hain,
Ek … khud ke muskurahat ke liye dusro ko kurban kar dena,
Aur dusra …dusro ke muskurahat ke liye khud kurban ho
jana.

(3)

Ki girte hue kabhi darna maat, Un ankho se ansu ko nikalne
dena maat, Halka sa muskurana, Aur kehna ……. Bahaut dur
ka manzil hain, Abhi to survad hain safar ko haseel karne ka.

(4)

Cheene ke jaise muskan hain uski,
Jispe dil phisla tha mera,
Aj bhi dukh ke badal rehte hain saath humare,
Par bhag jata hain woh sab jab saath rehta hain uska.

(5)

Kuch beete hue waqt gaam de jate hain, To kuch zakham, Par apno ke saath bitaye waqt, To humesha muskan e de jate hain.

(6)

Parayo se zyada to apno ne toda , Dil pe khanjar to apno ne dala, Phir bhi muskuraya, Aur kaha ……, Yeh akhri muskan hain, Iske baad to tumlog ke liye rone wala bhi koi nahi hoga.

Ketan B Jadhav

Ketan B Jadhav is passionate rider he is Founder and Director of his Company. He has comp leted his Graduation and diploma in computer.
He loves to go for adventure tours and enjoys the company of friends and slowly he has developed his writing talent too. He belongs to Maharashtra state and has been an inspiration for many.

Life is Long

Life is long
Full of song
Sometimes it's tough
But sometimes it's rough

In this beautiful world
Less people are curled
They make me fine
Even at dine

Among those few are near
Some are my dear
But I fear
As I dare not to lose dear

Someone is my life
Someone want to kill me with knife
Some want to care
That's okay and fair

Sometimes it's full of smile
With lot of style
Sometimes it's full of sugar
With spicy figure

Life is sometimes a lesson
Sometimes it's a session
It makes sometimes our fun
But not to worry about it just run

Life is long
Full of song
Sometimes it's tough
But sometimes it's rough .

Life Is Sugar with Smile

Life is sugar with smile
So adopt a new style
Don't be fragile
And just just smile

Life partner may be horrible
Some might be desirable
They too are hope
Don't tie them in rope

Live in fancy
With love and decency
Make life joyful
And as well colorful

In life relation are important
With lot of potient
It makes you cry
Don't lose just try

It might create bad luck
You make it good luck
You change the scene
With your smile scheme

Make caring habit
Don't share any rabbit
Just share your smile
Which will take your relation miles

Life is sugar with smile
So, adopt a new style
Don't be fragile
And just just smile

Keerthana

The Generous will prosper; those who refresh others for themselves will be refreshed Keerthana hails from Chennai, Tamil Nadu.A girl of sixteen running towards her dream, Full of Hope, finding her happiness in the smallest things. She's a blend of emotions trying to express it through her writings. She loves to be a hodophile and explore the world. She adds up with music which lights the world. Her main goal is to motivate people around her and spread positivity with smiles forever. She has accomplished great goals in sports,oratorical competitions and waiting for many more to attain the destiny. You can find her writings relatable @quotes_by_girly_writer

The First Love

Annie and Kate were close friends from their childhood. Everyone loves Annie and avoids Kate for his shabby look and for being very quiet. Annie loves Kate as everyone surrounded by Annie was talking always, irritating, and making fun of her. Kate uses to sit very calmly silently and watches all these. Once Annie fell down in the ditch and no one came to help her. Kate silently watched all these and gave his overcoat to help Annie and Annie went home happily. Annie told about Kate in his home and to her surprise, everyone wanted to meet Kate. After a day Annie met Kate in the park and told her that her parents wanted to meet kate and thank him for saving Annie. Kate accepted to meet and went to Annie's home with neatly dressed. There comes the turning point of the story. Kate enters Annie's home and Annie starts introducing everyone to Kate. Kate loved the gesture & the way they treated Kate in Annie's home. Everything was going great until Annie's dad returned from the office. Annie's dad's face suddenly changed terribly seeing Kate. Annie's dad remembered killing his mom and dad when he was 6 years old. Annie introduced Kate to her dad. Kate couldn't remember exactly but he felt that he has seen his face somewhere. Kate and Annie enjoyed being there and lov ed everyone. Kate was still thinking about Annie's dad. It was night 10 pm so Kate waved a bye and reached his home. He wanted to find who's is Kate's dad so he was looking at all his photo albums to see if he is there. He couldn't find Annie's dad's photo there.
The next day Annie and Kate met as usual. They started sharing their personals with each other and came to know very well. Annie came to know that Kate is abandoned and felt very bad for him. She promised that she would be with him till the last breath. Kate's eyes filled with tears hearing this. Kate was happy as he got a soul who cares for him finally. Days passed as Kate and Annie became thick and thin which made Annie's

father filled with fears and anxiety. He was the one who killed Kate's dad and mom in a car accident. But he couldn't share with anyone in his home. Things went as Kate and Annie started coming very often to Annie's home. Once Kate brought his childhood friend to Annie's home. Seeing Kate's dad he got shocked but he didn't tell anything or show anything. Annie's dad realized that his friend found him. He started scolding Annie and told her not to meet Kate henceforth. Annie couldn't figure out why Is her dad telling her not to meet Kate henceforth. Days passed as Kate started feeling abandoned and all alone. Annie became mad thinking about why dad hated him suddenly. Annie's mom passed away because of cancer. Annie couldn't bear the pain of losing her mother. She's deeply broken. After her mom's death, his dad became an alcoholic addict. Annie was all alone. In fact, she felt like killing herself. She started hurting herself every night which made her feel better. Days went and Annie's dad became very ill because of his alcohol. Annie was frozen for a second.

She doesn't even have money to treat her dad. She started to search for work all where. She met Kate's childhood friend in a cafe accidentally. She told everything to him and started enquiring about Kate. He replied that Kate is in deepest depression and he's under psychological treatment. Annie literally cried loudly in the cafe and everyone looked at her. He consoled her and took her to the psychological ward where Kate was admitted. Doctors strictly told not to allow anyone except Ron as he looks after Kate. Ron pleased the doctors for hours to make Kate and Annie meet. The moment when Annie met Kate, she hugged him with a loud wail. Kate couldn't figure what happened as he couldn't feel anything because of deep depression. He didn't react or not even utter a word. Annie kept wailing. The doctors told Annie that Kate is deeply depressed and he can't feel anything.

We're trying our best to recover him. Other than Ron we need someone who can talk regularly, change his mind and take him

somewhere where he loves to be. Annie told that she wants to talk to Kate for an hour. Looking at Annie's face the doctors couldn't refuse. They told them to talk to him slowly and call them immediately if he responds. Annie made Kate lie on his lap and started talking to him about the best days of her life which they both spent together. Annie could see tears rolling down from Kate's eyes.

Annie immediately called Ron and told him to rush up with doctors to meet Kate. Ron summons the doctor and takes Kate's room. Annie tells that look tears rolledfrom Kate's eyes. Doctors told her to keep talking without hurting them. It's a good omen that he's able to hear and let's hope for the best. Annie continues to tell how bad she felt losing her mom. Kate moved his hands and kept on her lap. Kate murmured "I taught, you would have married someone. Annie got a bit angrier and told him she can't think about anyone else except Kate. Kate murmurs that he waits to hold my hands. Annie tells him to let her wait for Kate's perfect recovery. Kate agreed and Annie g ave a warm smile. Suddenly her phone rings, Her neighbor Helen tells Annie that her dad is admitted to the hospital. Annie tells Kate and leaves the hospital immediately. Kate felt much better than before. Annie went to meet her dad. The doctors told themthat they need to treat him immediately.

He is in a very critical condition. She tries to collect money from her nearest and dearest and manages. The doctors told him that he is better but he holds his breath only for days. Annie promised that she would t ake care of him with utmost care. Annie got a job with the help of Ron and manages all kinds of stuff. Every day after work she spends time with Kate and the doctors told that he is doing great than before which gave Annie a ray of hope and positivity. Kate went to Annie's home to her dad. Annie says that she takes care like a born baby with deep grief. Kate consoles her and leaves back to Kate's home after months. Suddenly Annie's dad passed away.

Kate and Ron go to Annie's home. Kate holds her hand tighter and shows his all love to make her feel better. After few weeks Kate got a job and he decides to marry Annie. They were loving each other and starts living a happy life. Kate felt the warmth of his mother in Annie and Annie feels much secure and safer be ing with Kate. Kate realized that someone will definitely make us the happiest person and adds colors to our black and white portrait.

My World - My Bow Bow

How would I live without you
My bow bow, you're my precious sweetest companion,
The one who tolerates all my lements,
And enjoys listening them .

You look my eyes with deepest love,
Which humans failed to give,
And you taught me Dogs are better to Humans.

The way you cuddle with me and care me ,
Cannot be fulfilled by any human in the world
And I'm blessed to enjoy the way you love me.

I admire the way you bark,
When someone tries to get closer with me,
But no worries, My heart is already with you.
My love is only for you untill I live, my bow bow

Flairs and Glairs, a platform by a student for the students. We are esteemed youth struggling to carve out our path for our future and we follow a basic mindset Since everyone is not born with allround skills. Joining hands with people who are born to execute it with perfection is the best way to evol ve. Self-Evolution is the need of the hour but, evolving as a community is what we strive for.   The initiative as kickstarted by, Founder - Mr. Shubham Shah with the motive to utilize the skillset and talent of writing has now a team of 10+ people who are actively participating into newer forms of learning and discovering talents among youngsters. We Provide platform and services like Publishing opportunities, Open mics, Workshops, Hands-on training. Operating with Brand Name of Flairs and Glairs (Publication House), we offer the chance of elevating a passionate writer to an esteemed author   With Brand name Teekhe Zasbaaat. We bring to you an opportunity to get accustomed with the Public Speaking and Presenting of Thoughts along with regular challen ges to brush up your inking spirit.   The newest initiative to extend our services we introduced in a new writing Platform- The Glittering Fables and Ink Over Tears.

We Choose to Fly Like A Falcon than to be

a Leg Pulling Crab.

To Know More: Infoline – 7781900870
Mail Us At-
flairsandglairs@gmail.com / info@flairsandglairs.in
Or Visit is at
www.flairsandglairs.com / www.flairsandglairs.in
Social Handles- @flairsandglairs @teekhezasbaaat